I0567392

WHISPERS FROM BEYOND

A SHOWCASE OF DARK POETRY

Let the world know:
#IGotMyCLPBook!

Crystal Lake Publishing
www.CrystalLakePub.com

Copyright 2023 Crystal Lake Publishing

Join the Crystal Lake community today
on our newsletter and Patreon!
https://linktr.ee/CrystalLakePublishing

Download our latest catalog here.
https://geni.us/CLPCatalog

OUR LADY OF HOLY DEATH *Colleen Anderson*—Previously
published in the HWA Poetry Showcase IX, 2022

CRIMSON FACES *Maxwell I. Gold*—Previously published in
Space and Time Magazine, 2019

All Rights Reserved

ISBN: 978-1-957133-75-1

Cover art:
Kenneth W. Cain—www.kennethwcain.com

Layout:
Lori Michelle—www.theauthorsalley.com

WELCOME
TO ANOTHER

CRYSTAL LAKE PUBLISHING
CREATION

Join today at www.crystallakepub.com & www.patreon.com/CLP

TABLE OF CONTENTS

LOOK INTO THE CHRISTMAS BOX

AMABILIS O'HARA

See what I am made of you eager manchild
slavering for a peek
of the tissue-fleshed
present you stole

Your fingers ruck my wrappings
Twist my trappings
I am silent
when you shake me

Dig your thumbs in pleated pucker
purple paper slit
Dent my shape
Pry off my tape

Tear me bare with ragged nail scrape
Your tongue poking
index worms pink-prying
between bare lips

Hook my corrugated wrinkles
Spread me
like origami Goatse
perineum pinned back

1

Body a dead butterfly skin-bowed gift
blooming ribbons
sloughing sheets
from cardboard bones that crack

Open cavity steeped in deep hollows
My shadowed corners
stretch wide
to swallow men whole

Look into the box
See what I am made of

VILLANELLE FOR MONSTERS 101: DEMON MANAGEMENT

KB NELSON

It's hard to manage a demon, and dangerous while you find the
    way
to mastery. For one, you might speak sweetly lest its disposition
    curdle,
but you will find another needs a harsher word to make it stay

its claws and fangs, all while it thinks of you as prey.
You may have heard that love concoctions, strong with rose and
    myrtle,
can be useful. I advise, if compounding, that beginners steer away

from anything but calmatives. You can spot those braves who play
at demon love by their timeline of bruises: yellow, green, purple.
Knowledge of a demon's proper name's a mainstay

of old textbook lore. I loathe to be the one to naysay,
but this is not a useful avenue. Some names are nonverbal
in all respects. Humans—and indeed all mortals—have no way

in which to say the name. While you attempt to convey
the sense of appellation, you are turned to marble
or flames or a home in which the demon will choose to stay.

3

You have the chance to learn things I picked up the hard way.
Case in point: how to gain control is just your first hurdle,
chapter one of a long volume. Our upcoming lessons focus on the
    way
to maintain your hold. While hard to get, it's deadly if you don't
    make it stay.

CHILD OF ELEMENTS / SON OF SORROWS

AJ FRANKS

She breathes
Red wine's aroma
A transparent glass
Forever half-full
        He chokes
        On metallic air
        A sliver of glass
        Spills red on the floor
She sees
Not the dying star
But the wish within
Its immortal core
        He's blind
        To light from the star
        Crushed under pressure
        By its stellar core
She feels
Magic from the sea
Mermaid melodies
And seahorse secrets
        He's chilled
        Accursed by the sea
        Mermaid maladies
        And seahorse censures

She hears
Laughter in the wind
Whispering wonders
To those who listen
        He's deaf
        To cries of the wind
        Echoing caution
        Though he won't listen
She lives
Spirit of treasure
Heart, a dreamcatcher
And oh! How she loves
        He dies
        Body discarded
        Heart, broken-hearted
        And oh! How he loathes

THE TERRORS I BORE

TOM GULDIN

In deepest corners of my mind demons whispered
striving for control. I battled black shadows,
tormenting me, taunting me. Slowly I began to see
these demons were no mere fantasy.

Long-forgotten faces clawed at my sanity
as rending forms took shape,
phantasmal tooth and claw now solid,
no longer figments of my mind to escape.

I thought this pain illusory, now
demons once hidden laid bare,
spectral abominations made reality.
How could I have known the terrors I bore?

Secrets whispered, secrets long buried
secrets wished unknown, my reality unveiled,
unmasked before my waking mind.
I faced them—naked, weary, wounded.

COFFEE IN HELL

PIXIE BRUNER

We're going straight to hell
We stumble on bound/blistered feet at the cave,
We flip a coin to see who grips the blade and calls forth their father first,
grayer, thinner than of their blessed memories.

Called by blood on cold pebbles,
red droplets hibiscus petals on the grass
a splash of Manischewitz for mine,
a glug of Wild Irish Rose for yours, then are swallowed down.

Could we clasp hands,
maybe intertwine fingers
like intimate arachnids,
and converse,
to make the journey more pleasant?

If we pool all of our loose coins together,
maybe we can pay Charon
to row us across the Styx? Can we stop for coffee in Hell?
I hear they have sinfully good Devil's Food Cake.

Black bitter coffee, acrid and sharp daggers on the tongue.
Buttercream mortality pasting the moist layers together.
The coffee says "Noli frangere"—we inhale deeply anyway.
But please, do not look too closely at me.
I will not look at you. I cannot meet your eyes.
Neither of us are as beautiful as we once were.

Spices clogging our pores,
Nebulae cut into amuse-bouche,
given as samples from food stalls, comets
cold, crisp, snow cones falling apart on the tongue
No final destination planned,
Permanent tourists in the bizarre bazaar.

The music is relentless from the merry-go-round,
the polymer resin horses colicky
foam upon their scolding bridles,
and mad with bastard strangles.

Look ahead!
There is only forward, you have paid the fare, the fines, boarded
    the boat.
You forsook the cake even-
same with putting your eyes out.

No return trip for regret.
Leave it upon the dry shores and set it ablaze.
Watch the smoke and shades rise
from the crooked shore and falling sky,
with its stars and dreams and galaxies,
which is possibly ours now and forever and ever, worlds without
    end, amen.

GHOST BED

RHEA ROSE

Off the mattress
You rise, wake me with
your hollow wandering,
covered in cool sheets.

My fragments
fall low
you, behind me, bending
pressing pillows
With your dread,
Soft depressions,
Derange my sleep.

Shallow shadow
Creeping halls,
Come back to sleep,
Warm my cold stone feet.
Stop stealing slumber,
Coughing out
your sweet colognes.

Charred dark stain,
black steam,
wraith thing writhing,
nightmare wake,
Chewing black and bitter moons,
beneath bed's inhaling breath.

Stop spinning bedding
Driving darkness underneath,
Fleshy splintered tongues beneath,
soft white ash,
of dreams.

UNCHASTE VIRGIN

DIANTHE WEST

I catch the sound of my mother's sobs rushing alongside my fabric-
draped litter.
In my mind, I watch her tear at her red-clad breast as I pass.
My corpse robe, absent those ribbons and veils of class, signifies
my fel luck.
I'm a shame brought to market in a funerary parade.

Next to me, Valerie, all of five, was a gift, like myself, to the shrine.
She sits still, lost in thought, innocent, sweet pure child. I despair.
Our transport stops short. We jolt and we sway then keep on in our
dour politesse,
making our way to the Colline Gate, where we turn and then we stop.

Maids vow three decades of chastity; not knowing that it's a fool's
trade, yea—
th' empire has its way—stirring breasts, white orgies; now with
child.
The charge they bring me is lust unbecoming a vestal maid; I cry
guilt—
hand on the dagger tied flat to my thigh; a small mercy, oh!

Come to the gate, we process to the side of the catacomb vault and
arrest.
My little purse holds a small part of food and drink. Taking it,
Valerie breaks the small morsel in half, shares the greater part back
to me.
Is she naive? Or hastening death to her own angel self?

Inside the depth of the sepulcher vault stands a table, a lamp, and
a font.
Eight strong men bring up the ladder; they shut us up, shift the
earth.
Valerie waits, my companion in death—she's a senseless dear
sacrifice.
She takes the draft; she thirstily drinks and soon unknowingly
sleeps.

I pierce myself with the blade; a blood salvo runs through my
bronze curls like liquor.
Mine is a vision of Vesta, a vision of brazier lights.
I see the sea, a last glimpse of the cruor that flows blithely through
heaven and earth.
I've washed my sins clean, beat Hades—his malice is impotence.

DINING AFTER DARK

KATHRYN BURKETT

Devious creatures slither in shadows
silently creep upon unwitting revelers

the unbidden lull unsuspecting guests
into a dizzying waltz, whirling and twirling

perfumed hair discreetly brushed aside
revealing pale necks that demand attention

like a needle threaded red
sharpened fang slides into tender vein

a scene continuously replayed, new dancers
but the dance remains the same

sipping full-bodied wine like royalty
lording over still warm corpses

they are wild predatory progeny
playing under canopy of night

stalking and slaying instinctively
they delight in the carnage they create

suddenly ceasing and slinking away
before the first smear of sunrise

streaks across the sky, forcing their
unceremonious return to decaying tombs

'

THE ENCROACHING, ENDLESS NIGHT

ROGER TERRY

Why must the mind lie
Whilst the soul roars like thunder,
Is today a good day to die?

"No, it is not a good day," both moist, socketed globes deny.
Tears on the lidded rim yearn to spill, but pause to ponder,
Why must the mind lie?

Words catch, knot the throat, a tracheal tie.
The mind wrestles with yesterday's shadows, in wonder,
Is today a good day to die?

Once-unbearable contemplations pry,
Clawing the frontal lobes' door, intent on plunder.
Why must the mind lie?

Sanity's foundation teeters, its chains that bind belie.
The door gives way to reality, the mind opens to consider,
Is today a good day to die?

Finally, night takes hold. The end is nigh.
Tears fall, death drops its inevitable anchor.
Why must the mind lie?
Is today a good day to die?

BYZANTIUM CURSED

FAITH DINCOLO

She clings to her floral-flannel sheets
Hips ache because she will not turn
and face him

Fucking, his breath stinks of amber beer.
Dreaming now:

Nowhere leads to hacked out stairs
Lavender waves with stalactite fingers
crashes onto pyrite shores

washes through her coral toes.

Amethyst wind surrounds the girl
She licks a cherry lollipop
the paper stick unravels

clotting on her ruby tongue.

An ancient house buried in the thicket
fragrant rhodochrosite rosebushes strangle the dark porch
They creep and crawl with thorny awe.

Tears flood her floral-flannel sheets.

PLAGUE HAG

KT WAGNER

The plague hag returned. City condos for sale marked an exodus to suburbs, towns, and villages. A negligible commute when there's a network signal. Details worked out later.

Through history, mansion-like clergy homes crouched alongside church spires. A bell tower in every town, every village. The church wielded inordinate power.

City condo values declined. Country home values increased. Realtors nodded. Frowned. Latecomers to the migration, lowered expectations, open to possibilities.

The church preached conformity, adherence to roles and rules. Subservience to a God defined by men. Empires and institutions rose and fell.

A former church house, unoccupied more than a century. Requires renovation. Repairs. The intoxication of vast square footage. A silent garden. Blessed isolation.

Muttered rumour, ancient legends, curses. Warded by the sign of the cross. Houses shuttered against things which roam at night. Consecrated ground. Salted earth.

Tall tales the realtor claimed. Wild grains and grasses are healthy. Golden and eldritch purple seed heads ripe for harvest. Elbow grease. Sweat equity. A steal.

Everything of value in the parish houses auctioned off, buildings gutted. Sheets shrouded the remains. Rodents and spiders multiplied. Thrived.

A hearth fire crackled, incinerating the former occupants of the chimney. Cleaning and demolition first. Clear an area to sleep, an area to eat.

Local tradesmen refused work at the church house, warned off by fathers, uncles and brothers. Best leave it be. They muttered. Spat on the ground.

A wooden box sealed and buried. Mourning rings studded with teeth. Finger bones. A glass eye. Stained room behind a basement brick wall. Rusty tools, tatters of rotted fabric.

Enlightenment flowed and ebbed. Church membership plummeted. Rural populations fled for the city. The church divested. Hiding the sins buried beneath.

A glass eye dangled from a silver chain, its iris a storm-grey abyss. City friends tittered over flutes of chardonnay, homemade biscuits. Their dancing frenzied.

Reticent locals, wary of outsiders, maintain their distance. No talking. No shouting. Absolutely no singing. Or dancing. Move on quickly.

A screech of agony. An owl, not a human. A yowl. A cat, not a demon. Rabbits not unheard of. But there'd never been tell of one that big.

Warnings issued. Pagan healers, the full moon, seductresses, heretics, and sorcery. Keep women and girls inside. Under control. Education, power, opinions, all handled by men.

Whispers curled through keyholes. Mournful words tumbled, landed with a splat. Sour milk soaked into pounded chalk. Names. Birthdates. Occupations. Deaths.

Sidonia. Noblewoman, femme fatale. Beheaded and burned.
Agnes. Healer. Strangled and burned.

An ivy tunnel connected to a secret garden. Encircled in stone. Fed by a burbling spring. Sulphur, monkshood, belladonna, and water hemlock. Alluring. Deadly.

Anna. Servant. Decapitated.
Michée. Washerwoman. Hanged and burned.

Names spooled, curled, through cracks and vents. Landed in tangled clumps. A hardware store in the city sold a grey putty. Guaranteed to fix leaks and holes.

Bridget. Tavern owner. Hanged.
Sarah. Housewife. Mother. Hanged.

Shadows revealed a corner shelf no one could reach. Where there is no light, the silhouette of a poppet. Pinched. Choked. Bitten.

Outsiders never stayed long. The villagers knew this but never spoke of it, lest it draw unwanted attention.

Times passed. The plague hag gathered broom and rake, then retreated. Villagers mingled, cautious. Stories were spun of city dwellers who came and went.

Again, a realtor pounds a battered for-sale sign into the weedy lawn of the church house.

WHY I DON'T WRITE HORROR

MICHAEL H. PAYNE

Declare that doom and darkness dominate?
I quirk a brow. The concept lacks allure.
Conclusions soaked in bloody ruin grate
As much as schmaltz, banal and immature.

Excessive gloom and cheer will drive a spike;
Perspective-wise, I find them incomplete.
With optimists and pessimists alike
Convinced they're right, I think it's called "conceit."

Complaisance drips and saps the will away,
Creates a zombie feeling, clouds the mind.
Uncertainty's the stuff, the type of clay
I love to work no matter how maligned.

Rejecting both extremes, embracing doubt,
My goal's to delve, to stir, to play about.

PURSUED ON THE FERRY JESPER

BRIAN RICHARDS

I fled this way to the island Hven
Because I wanted the quiet of Tycho Brahe
I wanted to watch the lightning-sharp waves
Cut the space between us into orbits and math

But I see you back there watching
Having followed from the metro
Maybe to arrest me
Maybe there is pain to be had

So I chant and pretty for the gray monsters to rise
Out there all scale-backed and shining
And then I hold my breath against
The diesel fumes and metal fear. But not you

Your shadow waits behind me there
A silhouette among the seats
Like a balloon floating
Just above a quiet carnival

Like the moon sneaking
Up from the harvest corn
And instead of hay and the promised pie
I smell the muddy grave-fish about us

To hell and to pain and forget the scientist's solace
Enough with your accusations, your chase and taunt
The hints from the corners of my eye
At coffee, at the commercial break

End it with me here at the railing
Those slender wet beasts and their eyes
Like the coins of the sea
See in us only the crunch of our bones

While I admire the white rot on that wall

It occurs to me that heat has a smell
Like a hiding place or a secret room
Especially here at midday and hot autumn
I could chew on the warmth coming from these boards

I could chew on the hot bony history
Of this house where they say families died
Where a fire or a phantom or a madman
Or three or four kinds of boogey ghoul waited for prey

And when I sit here in what must have been a parlor
Up to my knees in the rotting upholstery
Of what must have been a couch (or is that davenport?)
My sweat mingles with the noise of those heat scents and legends

Stay put and let me tell you how ghosts will move in daylight
Breaking glass, breaking plaster, chasing and scaring
And how there is no pain coming from their canvas and pinpoint
     eyes
They eat you in moments of surprise

They eat you in these moments while I have you prisoner
So I can tell you about the stomps of king kitchen hammer
Maybe show you where he stuffed ghosts in this little pile of fabric
Cooking in this cicada scented heat so you have friends while you
     stay

JUST BEYOND THE LIGHT

TOM DEADY

Crows whisper in the night
Lining the trees and wires
Always just beyond the light

Memories fade from sight
Dreams forgotten by daybreak
Crows whisper in the night

Some wrongs can't be made right
Secrets and betrayals, love gone cold
Always just beyond the light

No chance to reunite
Cuts won't heal, scars won't fade
Crows whisper in the night

Tattered remains of a love once bright
Broken promises, shattered dreams
Always just beyond the light

Flapping wings, birds in flight
Shadows joined, now broken
Crows whisper in the night
Always just beyond the light

DEMONS FOLLOW ME

RAE YOUNG

they sulk slither shapeshift to fit their mood
life's traumas animated to shadow my every move

some days one wraps around my leg
like a needy toddler driven to beg
demanding attention with increasing screams
searing my insides
with life's never-ending experiences

demons follow me

we exist together forever
as long as I desire to continue my breath

no deal made beget their haunting
traveling life together was never our desiring
but my demons are children never cared about
I am the guardian of their hideouts
a parent to hear fears and doubts

demons follow me

sometimes we sit and hide from life
most times we trudge on through and survive

my demons permeate every part of me
I must lead until we find our final peace

THIS HOUSE

K. D. BOWERS

An evil spirit haunts this house,
Yet no one believes me.
Floorboards creak, candles flicker and fade.
I hear my sister scream, and then, dead silence.

No one believes me.
Razor sharp claws and glowing ruby eyes at the top of the attic
    stairs—
I hear my parents scream, and then, dead silence,
Except for the ringing, ringing in my head, and thumping in my
    heart.

Razor sharp claws and glowing ruby eyes at the cellar stairs—
A dance of dread sways inside my worried mind.
Ringing, ringing in my head, and thumping in my heart.
I hide and dare not to make a sound.

A dance of dread spins around my worried mind.
My sister's flesh is torn apart, bones snap.
I hide and dare not to make a sound,
And all hope withers, like leaves in smoke.

My parent's flesh is torn apart, bone is broken.
An evil spirit haunts this house.
All hope withers, like leaves in smoke.
Floorboards creak, candles flicker and fade.

CREEPS ON THE TOPMOST FLOOR

Melissa Stauffer

On the topmost floor
At the end of the hallway
The very last door.

No one should be passing at the a.m. of four
Not even the creeping light of dawn
On the topmost floor

Dark of night emphasizing lines around the door,
the peephole glimmers as if someone passes the way
Of the very last door.

Shadows busy with some strange chore,
But no one needs on this path their feet to lay
On the topmost floor

Something has creeped up to the door
Persistent knocking heard halfway
At the very last door

Yellow light continues through the bluish hue to pour
In a shudder you wildly sway
On the topmost floor
The very last door
Whiled Away Whimsy

Whimsical whimsy whirring in the dark
Why why why the repeating cry
Whispers and wakefulness hiding in the shadows
Weary weary traveler, come rest your head here

Lightning swarms across the sky
Whips and wills and wailing wax
Whittling wishes for whismsy away.
Peaceful travels writhe in weather awry

Wistful hopes lance the heart.
Will the victor truly gain the spoils?
Writhing shadows in the dark.
Haunt the head that wanted rest on the pillow.

THE ROUSING

CHRIS P. CLAY

Awakened by the dawn
and giddy robin giggles
I emerge into the gray light
with my loyal hound companion
and venture forth to explore

Sinking into mossy murk
I bear witness to the stirring
In the croon of distant peeper frogs
drooping boughs weep without shame
Footsteps squelch in the loam

Observe the primal secrets
exposed by melting snow
Bits of bone, fur and feather
Green leathery fingers sprouting
through molding leaves like shed skin

Trudge deeper onward
Away from the guarded world
Each cautious, careful tread
sends unseen life skittering
While the waking master writhes beneath

AWAY

JEM KRAS

his hands' scarlet outlines
seared into my skin

Come, oh Mother, take me away
Om Dum Durgayei Namaha

sharp cloud of scotch surrounds him
step-Mom stands at the side

om dum durga
om dum durga

run to safety, into closet
slam the door, hold the knob

om dum durga
om dum durga

bottom to floor
feet to frame

Om dum durga
Om dum durga

stomps outside
jiggles knob

Om dum Durga
Om dum Durga

bang Bang
Bang Crack

Om Dum Durga
Om Dum Durga

YOU GET THE
FUCK OUT HERE

OM DUM DURGA
OM DUM DURGA

She's coming for me
in here, I'm in here

BANG thud—

       —crack the door open
       darkness—trucker hat abandoned

       I am still here
       She came not for me

DON'T CRY

KAREEM HAYES

The Little boy sits silent
Hiding behind corner of his mind
Every night the demons arrive
Every morning the monsters awaken

"Good mourning,
Sunshine."

Sunup he fights to open his eyes
Welded close by mucous neglect calcified
Sundown he fights, to close them, frozen open
Sheer terror
Run to the mirror, Re-remember
Is this face, still his face?
The iris entry to a black hole
A window into a tainted soul

"Pull down your pants"
"You better not cry! . . . Either"
"If you cry you get more.
I will give you something to cry for!"

Daydream
A tear escapes
He kills it quickly
 the art of suicide
The art of dying alive
After all who can hurt you.

Worse than you?
"Don't Cry"
He whips himself
36 inches of cow hide
whips himself
36 lashes until he
The Little boy sits silent
Hiding behind corner of his mind
Every night the demons arrive
Every morning the monsters awaken

"Don't Cry"
"DONT . . . Cry"
"What the hell is wrong with you! What are you doing?"
"Teaching my host not to cry."
"What?! Take your little dumb ass to bed!"
"But that's when the Demons come."
Monsters don't believe in Demons.
But Demons believe in Monsters.

The Little boy sits silent
Hiding behind corner of his mind
Every night the demons arrive
Every morning the monsters awaken

Night falls, Lady Luna rises casting rays of silver pixie dust
He can't picture his face in the twilight
He can't remember his own face in twilight
But he can recall what the demons look like . . .

They scratch & claw their way in
Feasting on the entrails of his fears
Delighting in his anxiety
Frolicking to the pitter patter of his tiny heart
His nervous sweat quenches their thirst.
The faceless figures taunt his rest
"Don't Cry" they utter with sinister grins
"No one will believe you not even the monsters."

 . . . Don't Cry.

CORPSE WHISPERS

AN EXQUISITE CORPSE POEM BY THE POETS OF AUTHOR'S JOURNEY

Dancing to the music of a lone cricket chirping [*Michael H. Payne*]
Billowing fog dances around me, I watch as the ships slowly drift
   out into the abyss. The call of the void beckons me, her words
   wrap around my soul and pull me into everlasting darkness.
   [*K. D. Bowers*]
Unsung songs hang in the air like timid ghosts [*Kathryn Burkett*]
silver susurrations disrupt the silence [*Jem Kras*]
Sighs devour obsidian seams I dreamed to sever the sky [*Amabilis
   O'Hara*]
A cackle of lilies strike in the cold. Their fetid flushes unfurl upon
   me. [*Dianthe West*]
The voice calls out, words trite yet true, heartbreak of old rising up
   from the darkest hue. [*Roger Terry*]
throw the tea, an apple, spear an oar, the stapled ears, at the knotty
   pine to silence the sibilance. [*Pixie Bruner*]
Click, clack. Click, clack. Ghostly needles knit our shroud [*KT
   Wagner*]
These fierce vibrations wound the frightening. [*Rhea Rose*]
A breeze beyond the grave suffused with fading sounds of suffering
   [*AJ Franks*]
the susurrant hush, dissonant quiet sweeping through the
   cemetery [*Melissa Stauffer*]
. . . nose open to the breeze, I catch the delectable scent of your
   liver . . . [*KB Nelson*]

Perhaps we'll all be more temperate, to it and tender when we've
    withered down to bones. [*Chris. P. Clay*]
One thing I will keep to remember. [*Angela Yuriko Smith*]
Echoes of souls lost to our sight their cries interweave, a requiem
    of night. [*Tom Guldin*]

MY SIBLINGS WERE BURIED LIKE GOLDFISH

AMABILIS O'HARA

Radiation sick
Mom dumped my oldest sister
down the soiled toilet

Her body to blame
she closed red-rimmed eyes to flush
her second child too

She tells me the tale
wailing mantras of *they're gone*
I do not agree

Kneeling on cold tile
I light candles on the rim
and pray to porcelain

Dank death gods listen
Twin spirits gurgle back up
like bloody sewage

Don't cry Mother dear
I soothe as I fish for flesh
Plunk souls in wet womb

My found siblings float
in the bowl of Mom's belly
as I feed them flakes

RABBIT PUNCH

KT WAGNER

Grandma murmurs, *rabbits, rabbits, rabbits.*
Monthly, awakening's first utterance.
The Fates teach guarded habits,
Always spurn unthinking sufferance.

Rabbit, bunny, hare, thirty days of luck.
Three Graces, three cheers, a three-ring circus,
A witch—the white hare—seeks prey, moonstruck.
A curse is but a wish come full circle.

Ride a hare's tail to marriage, Grandma said.
Lepus zigging, zagging, from Orion's
Pack a flaming torch refusal to wed.
My heart's desire—a loop of dandelions.

The Furies emerge from drops of my blood.
Rabbits, rabbits, rabbits, a lucky blight.

WHAT THE ANTS ARE SAYING

MICHAEL H. PAYNE

Sometimes when I'm working,

the ants'll get into my head.

Unpleasant? Not as such, I must admit

Compared to other pests my fevered brain

Has wrought and wrangled. Ants appear to fit

With little bother, hardly any pain.

But still, I mean, well, *look!*

They rea range stuff, turn su jects

to obje ts, unp c thin s I've

d finite y acked, upset the delic te

tructur s of my thought proc sses—

bring cake please

Actually, I wouldn't mind some cake... *

39

TONIGHT'S SUPERHERO

BRIAN RICHARDS

A time traveler
This time I will be an owl
A fluttering knot
Of flying predator

Landing hard
Chilled talons first
Rushing into view with wings wide

I'll visit then after dark
When the fall leaves in 1984
Had life in their scent

I'll arrive with a whoosh and
A cry of havoc because
Nature's heroes do that, don't they?

And Thirteen Year Old Me
Will grow still
In fear and awe

Because I remember now I always loved owls
And wished them as friends

Without words I'll scare away the demons
My owl eyes will be enough comfort until the dawn

And Thirteen Year Old Me
Will not sit awake afraid tonight

NOTHING PERSONAL

MICHAEL H. PAYNE

The morning's crystal blue drip-dries the overnight clouds away while I tromp the usual mile to work at the library. My steps stumble, though, when a crow somewhere nearby shotgun-scatters a blast of staccato static. Caw-caw-cawing from the house on my left, the bird swoops to light on the next lamppost, its feathers bristling, its body crooked toward me, its cursing continuous. I creep past, and it shoots ahead overhead to the tree at the corner. No one else in sight, I cross beneath, and the crow's clatter follows me down the street till the echoes fade, fade, fade in the distance.

Along that same block, the crow harangues my evening return. The next morning, too, and the next evening, the next morning, the next evening.

Averting my eyes, hunching my shoulders, wracking my brain: what did I do? What did I do?

foulness incarnate,
all humans presumed guilty,
murderers of crows!

LUST

AJ FRANKS

A nightmare I'd like to have repeatedly!
I adore spiders. I find them completely fascinating and terrifying, yet majestic in both appearance and action. My obsession has officially grown deeper after reading "The Boy With The Spider Face" by AJ Franks. A story of acceptance, revenge, and a plethora of body horror, this novella was a dream to read and by that I mean a nightmare that I want to have repeatedly. AJ Franks explores several very real social issues through the eyes of a phenomenal main character attempting to figure himself out, while surrounded with abhorrent characters who idolize their own ideas of "normal" and demonize anything outside of those created parameters while forming and maintaining divides. The pressure starts from the very first page and gradually builds until the reader is caught in a tight web, both begging for their life and dying to see what's waiting in the dark, knowing that the only relief is turning the page. Even the most modest of horror readers will find themselves rooting for the well written carnage made imperative to the story by a plot seeking to provoke and viciously bite. "The Boy With The Spider Face" won't ever let you forget.

A nightmare to
adore

A
body to
explore

to
idolize
and demonize while
maintaining divides. The pressure starts
and builds caught in a tight
web, begging for life and dying to
know relief Even the
modest

bite.

THE GEOMETRY OF BOTANY

KB Nelson

"Keep it cool," our battle cry,
"transpiration not perspiration!"
and so high-rises, office buildings
rectangular homages to concrete and steel
softened their edges

we webbed and latticed walls
festooned with moss and lichen
green and white as Christmas
decorated with the blood of our blisters
we laid fecund earth over roofs
seeded   watered   waited

walls rounded   browns greened
with sprouts and leaves
smiles shared   backs patted
audacious as a wart

the first collapse was an anomaly
the second, a concern
the third, a panic
as a pattern
emerged

the weight of life
descended to the streets
unwilling to be party

to this shroud of deceitful greenery
over rude squares and unseemly angles
we are now peacefully surrounded
chunks of concrete   steel   lattice   earth
and broken bodies to fertilize it all

BORNE UPWARDS FROM THE SEA

DIANTHE WEST

The Bentley roars down the rocky drive.
Lured phantoms loom over, black and white.
Infrared leaves clatter under the moon.
The iron gate's barred.
Trees turn.
A change in nature,
tenacious, secretive, silent.

These desolate days
are the sound of crashing waves.
They shimmer underwater,
in a din, a mighty swell
of ever-changing expressions.

Out on the beach,
her nose detects a sweet scent.
Her leather-gloved hand
finds a sketchbook on the shore,
a soaked cashmere sweater,
a dripping diamond bracelet,
tender curls at the nape of a neck,
broken like mandarines.

She bends down,
takes the neck in her hand,
wipes the salt from her lips,
the light taste of smoke.
Forgive me.

LOCH ALLURE

CHRIS P. CLAY

Limpid lantern lamplight seeps
across the inky dappled depth
failing to illuminate, revealing
what lurks beneath the swell

Across the inky dappled depth
shush, gurgle and foam
What lurks beneath the swell
o'er which the vessel cleaves

Shush, gurgle and foam
Searching, twin oars pierce the surface
o'er which the vessel cleaves
Tonight their carnal clandestiny

Searching, twin oars pierce the surface
Gaze returned across the ripplet
Tonight their carnal clandestiny
Her piscine heartbeat thrums

Gaze returned across the ripplet
Fair face, liquid hair framing fish eyes
her piscine heartbeat thrums
tail twitches iridescent imbrication

Fair face, liquid hair framing fish eyes
Webbed fingers offered upward, glistening
tail twitches iridescent imbrication
She sings her song of beguiling

Webbed fingers offered upward, glistening
beckon into the ebony wetness
She sings her song of beguiling
Sever terra's bond as the boat sways farewell

Beckon into the ebony wetness
Into tight embrace, full of triumph and hunger
Sever terra's bond as the boat sways farewell
with underwater kiss — taste of iron and algae

Limpid lantern lamplight seeps
across the inky dappled depth
failing to illuminate, revealing
what lurks beneath the swell

FROST AND FLAME

MICHAEL H. PAYNE

Penelope's heard so much about
the fire of creativity, about
the artistic urge that burns and churns
throughout a person's insides.

But as a piano-playing penguin,
she's never felt that sort of thing at all.
The only burning and churning inside *her*,
she's noticed, comes from eating too fast.

Still, sitting at her keyboard,
she wonders, practicing her scales—
no fish jokes, if you'd be so kind—
what the fire of creativity feels like.

Settling in to play, she recalls
cold, clear afternoons when the
sky and ice seem to merge,
each as blue and white as the other;

mornings when the sun doesn't rise
for days, and the notes and chords
she sends out ring like crystal bells
under the sharp, crackling stars;

evenings that go on and on and on,
the light frozen glinting in place
to hold back the night from ever arriving.
These animate her flippers and her music.

Aubades, ballades, serenades, nocturnes,
all crisp as frost, devoid of flame:
neither she nor her audience
would want it any other way.

REQUIEM FOR LOST SOULS

TOM GULDIN

~after Wilfred Owen—*Anthem for Doomed Youth*

"I hate war as only a soldier who has lived it can, only as one who
has seen its brutality, its futility . . . " ~*Dwight D. Eisenhower*

What otherworldly requiems announce the passing of these souls,
solely the unleashed fury of cursed weaponry,
only the faltering volleys from arcane patrols
can utter their hurried supplications in swift delivery.

No entreaties, no tolls, no vestige of scorn remains,
merely the unhinged chorus of keening projectiles
and bugles summoning them to desolate campaigns—
malevolent beacons hastening their voyage into exile.

Clasped solely in youthful gazes proud
they radiate mystical whispers of departure.
Maidens shall cloak them within ghostly shrouds,
their wreaths—empathy from decayed legislators.

In fading twilight they plummet, victims of brutality,
leaving behind only echoes of sorrow and futility.

SALT, CARAMEL, CHOCOLATE

DIANTHE WEST

Plunge our hands into winter's salt.
December's visits bring caramel.
Our childlike eyes seek Constance, her chocolate;
and perils buried 'neath the rose garden.
Through frosted glass panes of the library,
we slow-roasted ghosts crave sweet books.

Devils and angels are traced in our books.
We temper their voices with milk and salt.
Twelve seasons we've haunted the library,
scared the boy who makes the caramel;
raised our souls from snug beds in the garden;
under hazel-piped pin-leaves of chocolate.

Nights, Constance works the chocolate.
By day, she molds books.
Bakes her cakes from rich layers of the garden;
from the sounds of our deaths—half cacao, half salt.
Our ganache-filled ghosts long for caramel.
We shelve our gold foils in the library.

Tonight, a sugar bloom creeps through the library.
Its moist, fel mouth answers only to chocolate.
Its rich breath a sweet scent of caramel;
it's a luscious burnt custard of books.
Connie sets down her conching; she sniffs at the salt,
darts down spiral-coin steps to the garden.

Our velvety souls infuse her in the garden.
With Constance suffused, we melt up to the library.
Through candy framed windows, we're pouring out salt.
Our laughs taste like chocolate.
Our dead letters coat the books,
like craven roses of caramel.

Out on the drive, in a carriage full of caramel,
lights a buttery bird from our garden.
She croaks out gold wrappers for all of the books.
Pipes the name of the library;
Puffs her plundering cheeks in chocolate—
ploughed fields; she sings of boneyard salt.

Indulge in rich caramel, a decadent house of books!
Our drizzled salt garden's a spectral spice treasure
of silver-wrapped solstice in the chocolate library.

BABY FOOD

Rhea Rose

Chef picked my child,
Plucked ripe baby fat boy
From umbilical vines,
Dusted cradle cap
From his scalp,
Poured lotions
From tall Balsamic,
Vinegar bottles,
Oils over baby's bald head.
Lay him in a bed of lettuce,
bocconcini ball cheese
for a pillow,
Lemons sliced to transparency
Decorated a salty plate, cherry tomato
over each eye,
Basil toes.

Handed fork and knife,
Prepared to dine on
Infant endive,
Sucking up the savoury scents,
Spicey, pepper, earthy fleshy
folds of chubby chin.

My nostrils whiffed chef's
Alcoholic aftershave on my salad son
Disappointed, I sent back my meal.

RECONNAISSANCE OF THE SECOND MOON OF THE FOURTH PLANET

KB NELSON

```
                clods                    defy gravity
  sky islands        chunks              defy expectations
    amaze explorers           serene pieces of
      floating forest


            air-anchored
            fascinate researchers           roots dangle in
                                            shade below

LTA
    craft
rise                                            silent
        study                                       work as
        sample                                  prehensile
        test            roots                       roots
        air cars        trail                       grasp
      hover             stretch                  the
                analysts        reach &          craft
      enter             curl                     no
    data                around                   ears
          in               unmindful             to
            logs           vehicles                  hear
                           & their                the
                         pre-                      metal
                           occu-                   & glass
```

pied   crunch

cont-   no-one
    ents   to take
    -               note
              of

                              the
                          screams

    sky islands
              hang in the air

calm   look like
        patient   invitations
    well-nourished

                  whet &
    refine their
    appetites

THE DANCE

K. D. BOWERS

Dead girl
Dances at dawn
Twirling, swirling, swaying
The living drop dead from her curse
Revenge
A cruel prank, sealed her fate
Love once pure, turned
To dust

TOMORROW'S WINTER

JEM KRAS

the girl turns squealing
snow boots, coat, and gloves ready
carrot nosed men glow
from nuclear winter ash
oh eternal wonderland!

THE HUES OF DARKNESS

TOM DEADY

I
want
people
to know me.
That I'm capable
of going beyond the shadows.
My twilight is many colors.
it's the white of bone,
sightless eyes,
greying
flesh

RAIN FALL

ROGER TERRY

rustic eyes witness
the deluge batter the trees
tears drowning the past

THE HANGMAN

AJ FRANKS

He came upon a damp and burdened forest.
No witness save the voyeuristic crows.
The lassoed bough creaked
(a haunting bon voyage),
and crickets paused in silence
as duff failed to meet his toes.

INTIMACY

JEM KRAS

raw resplendent bear
guts and devours body
my heart untouched

THE DEVIL SAVED MY DAUGHTER

K. D. BOWERS

You put me in this body,
And now, torment is all these eyes
Will ever know—nothing more . . .
I am a good soul who means no harm
I made a deal with you
To save my dying daughter

Nothing in the world means more than my daughter.
Until I taken 100 souls, I am trapped in this body,
For this task I must complete for you
Is to gouge out men's eyes
And instill sheer fear.
My burden, heavy as the ocean's depths, I can bear no more.

My victims bleed more
And I think of the brightness of her world, oh, how my daughter
No longer has to suffer harm
From the disease that infected her body,
Starting with her eyes.
Now, she is safe and sound because of you.

All I hear is laughter from you
As I hesitate to lodge the knife deeper
Into this victim's eyes.
He is the same age as my daughter.
My hand trembles as I take in the bloody body—
I strive to avoid causing further harm.

As I depart from the scene, an officer firmly seizes my arm.
"Monster! How dare you?"
The officers shout as they turn away from the body
My duty is not finished, for I must kill more.
My thoughts are ever with you, my dear, beloved daughter,
And my heart frail, I weep from covered eyes.

The city peers into my soul through my eyes
A never-ending battle, I have caused so much harm—
Yet, they will never understand how it was all for my daughter.
I am strapped in the electric chair as you
Whisper into my ear, "You should have killed more."
Bolts of electricity race through my body.

DEATH SHUFFLE

RHEA ROSE

His shiny shoe clicks a door,
Her red dead toes drag on floors,
Pushing shushing, narrow halls,
Head hair tangles, wooden floor,
Stiff sweet skin falls white creep sleep,
Rolling death light lacy gore,
nightgown twists her torso up,
heaps, resists, slides
down lightless corridor,
dead breath wrapped grey silk plush,
pushing fleshing death crossed floors,
pushing shushing rolling doors,
shoving foot down dim floors,
rolling brushing velvet walls,
stuffing satin round cornered halls,
pushing shoving splinters gore
wooden white limb touches floor
reposing whispering moans remorse,
dark nest hair mass halos head.
Pushing shuffling down
narrow halls, death shuffle, shuffling
pushing black ward,
velvet walls.

MURDER PARADOXIA

PIXIE BRUNER

Noir—
dark places, white jazz.
Clock for a heart
Books of blood.
Holed up with a helpless lush,
I married Rasputin.
(Confidential paradoxia)

For lunch, it was the
The Blue Hammer, pure pulp,
juicy sweet forbidden strange fruit,
the wall through the road.
For dessert —
The ~~Dain dame~~ damn curse was big knowledge.

The continent of the street corner
The blonde—
Black Friday—
The moon shoots the piano player.
Post-literate wonderland
High-culture electric gumbo.

Fear and loathing of endless love
The man in the woods said "Farewell my lovely."

From the high window of murder,
that big sleep after that long goodbye
The grifters heed the thunder.
Now, and on earth—
Nothing more than murder.

//

A man of mucho mojo in a vanilla ride
cockfights another woman chaser
In the shark-infested
custard mountains of madness.
The exegesis of someone owes me money,
The zap gun, please, Dr. Bloodmon(k)ey . . .

Masks of the Illuminati fall off—
to reveal Schrödinger's cat
eating a naked lunch.
Guilty secrets from the chocolate war, flow my tears,
"The body was found in lot 49" the policeman says.
Travels, unnaturally cold in July—
now wait for last year.

THIS OCCASION CALLS FOR FLOWERS

KATHRYN BURKETT

Another boldly colored bouquet
clutched in the fist of a blushing bride
All pretty things are doomed to decay

Weeping woman on her wedding day
blossoming bump she struggled to hide
another boldly colored bouquet

Her life unfolds like a tired cliche
too weak to prevent it, though she tried
All pretty things are doomed to decay

Constrained like a puppet in a play
though she desired to cast aside
another boldly colored bouquet

Bitter her story ended this way
Harsh truths of life cannot be denied
All pretty things are doomed to decay

She's sleeping now. Nothing more to say
Stone cold at the scene of suicide
Another boldly colored bouquet
All pretty things are doomed to decay

THE TRULY DANGEROUS LIAISON

PIXIE BRUNER

Surely, you know that poets only wind up killing each other
or even more ironically, themselves.
Two poets together is polyamory
never fair or satisfying—
the words always want more,
and/or the spouse less.

There is always competition.
Every moment, every conversation,
every bowl of alphabet soup, silence, or spoken word
is Mirandized

They shall and will be used against you,
at the dinner table,
the public reading
or a court of law.

Poets are not safe with each other.
The poetess is best off with someone for
whom words are not the business,
the Sirens, the klaxons, the calling,
Strikethroughs are serial killers.

Lithoromantic if too happy-
Limerence for the word of the day.
Best off with someone for whom Zelda is just a
video game princess. (IYKYK, he says)

Noun verb. Noun verb. Noun verb.
Adjective noun verb. Adjective noun verb preposition noun.
Pronoun expletive exclamation mark.

Word games turn to mind games.
    Summer lawns become "dog salads,"
  Metaphor becomes meta-4,
    a discussion of "counting derangements"
gets personal.

We hail Eris like Ubers.
the car alarms screeching as
objects hurled from their solar systems,
Paperweight meteors, coffee mug comets,
Shooting scissors, chapbook planets.
The children of poets are stillborn some way.
Born under bad constellations. Mixed genetic metaphors.
Black horoscoped, that evil star where rats live.

When one takes up a pencil of pen or stares at the unforgiving
cursor for hours
 reproductive organs should be plucked and burned like love letters
and engagement portraits in Weber grill crematoriums.

There are too many letters written
    (some never sent) between poets
        like Discordian apples.

The poets, their seeds, these words,
    will force feed each other until these
over engorged deer ticks "POP!"
    and always leave the pages . . .

too
damn
empty!!!

SHADOW SHACK

CHRIS P. CLAY

It emerges with the dying light-
A tiny house of two stories
perched upon four carriage wheels
and tucked against the curb
of a sleepy neighborhood
A single bare lightbulb
blazes in one lone window

With no tow at the hitch
no sign of life inside
Who can say how it got there
or to whom it belongs
Resting disharmoniously
'neath the terrace maples
It loiters balefully till morning

Like a package left in anonymity,
wrapped in soot gray vinyl siding
the shadow shack confounds
Disturbing in its foreignness
Incongruous amongst such cultivation
Like a burr beneath the leather
it irritates and chafes

Its malignant presence agitates
destabilizing the status quo
of the once peaceful suburb

The otherness and perceived threat
a patent omen of things to come
Eliciting indignant protest
uttered in embarrassed tones

Still no one dares
report the rattling anomaly
Guilt and shameful bias hold sway
While bitter dread swirls
inside of cocktail glasses
and ice cubes of apprehension
dilute the companionable accord

By dawn the shed is vanished
Leaving nothing save a pall
Where once a home of vibrance stood
A desiccated domicile slouches
All hollow husk and melancholy
A repellent void in a once brilliant smile
Subject to whisper and perturbation

LAKE BABY

FAITH DINCOLO

Early upon sunlight's waking
Crows so still their beaks don't caw
Cries upon the water's edge
A translucent child wanders alone

She stumbles on the rocky beach
Her round belly wobbles
Beneath her pink ruffled swimsuit
The same one she drowned in

Her cries echo upon the lashing shore
Lake Baby cries for a momma
Whom she wants to suckle with her
Sharp, cold teeth

BON(E)FIRE

AMABILIS O'HARA

snap
split spook
spine on your shin
clack
cursed bones
ringed in singed stone
pssh
sprinkle
salt butane straw
chhk
sulphur
match strokes a jaw
sizzle
sear skin
flick the flame in
whoosh
hell heat
final defeat
crack
crispy
marrow swells sweet
pop
bursts the
wicked wight

TOMORROW, I'LL BE FIVE

JAMAL HODGE

Inspired by Pulitzer Prize-winning photo "The Vulture and the little Girl" by Kevin Carter, 1994.

My skin is gaunt,
       drawn tight to the skull.
My eyes are wide.
If I can make it,
Tomorrow, I'll be five.

No one will celebrate,
No one is left alive.
   The tall men opened dad
To show us the pink stuff under the red.
   Mom ran and lost half her head.
I gathered as much as I could carry of her in my pocket,
Before they sent me on my way.
The whole village was on fire.
The tall men said, "Have a nice day."

It gets hot out here.
   I drank from the water on the floor.
My stomach got sad,
   it hurts so bad,
I miss my mom,
I miss my dad.

Things are coming out of me,
In colors very bold.
Greens and browns,
Whites, and sticky gold,
They explode from my nose
   down my legs,
   from my frown.
The colors follow me
As I crawl across the ground.

What's the sun doing,
   why won't it go away?
It does things to my skin.
   It peels away.

Everything hurts.
   The flies are the worst.
   It seems they're here to stay.
Maybe they've come to celebrate?
My birthday is just a day away.

Sometimes the world goes off
      and comes back again.
I reach out and eat what I can.
      Dirt is salty,
      has no taste.
The predators who've seen me
Think I'm a waste.
Hard to move.
Easy to count my ribs.
I want to be five,
      but I wonder if I'll live.

Tomorrow, I'll be five.
      Where's Mom?
      Where's Dad?
I want to go where they are,
I want to go away.
I think I'm almost there.
The sudden sound makes me stay.
Thunder on the ground,
The sound of feet.
      People to meet.

I turn my head,
      it's all I can do.
Mom, Dad, is that you?

There's a man, pale as milk,
      and others too.
They look very sad.
      Are they hungry too?
I want to warn them to get away.
The tall men might come,
      to take important things away.
Rid them of their smiles,
Their pointing fingers
And curious glances.
Light flashes from the rectangles in their hands.
Some cry, none help.

My skin is gaunt,
      drawn tight to the skull.
      My eyes are wide.
If I can make it,
Tomorrow, I'll be five.

CRIMSON FACES

MAXWELL I. GOLD

Originally published in Space and Time Magazine (2019)

Wandering along the floor of a dying wood, I found strange comfort in the faceless of the night. The empty stars above flickered with a happy dread as the dried leaves, sucked entirely of their greenery, crunched under my leather boots. I could not recall what alien force brought me to this place, but whatever it was, the immensity of the thing in the air weighed down on my thoughts in a way that I could not reasonably discern. An obscure feeling, like that of some opaque rusty matter, seething through my veins. Dust and fog clouded my vision as I followed the dirt road towards a shadowy place. I left the station some time ago, months maybe. Years, even. Again, those platitudes escaped me as did everything else. The Phlegmatic God had taken what was left of my faulty idealism, drenched in a wretched coat of falsehoods, only to soak it in the bitter stench of my new reality, oozing with crimson pus. There ahead were the ruins of a dead society, one built in the great cyber forges where silver flames belched new stars, and birthed innovations so wild, men were said to be driven insane with joy. Though, a figment of that city was all that remained, a figment and an empty train station with the burning red hunger racing towards it with an unwilling haste propelled by that phlegmatic beast whose thirst for an unremitting darkness which fueled its wild locomotion.

Pale sprigs and upturned roots passed by my window as the train barreled onward. I smelled the foul odors coming off the petrified wood in the form of some grotesque fungi, mixing with the rusty hinges. My senses militarized themselves in an attempt to counter the offending stenches, but their campaign was thwarted for the odors were too strong; and my eyes were still muddled with a pustule horizon of iron and blood, only to be reckoned by guttural noises coming from outside the speeding train. The mob of red faces flowed precariously close to the tracks like some sinister music, scored to the backdrop of burning trees and ashy skies, screeching, bleeding with an electrified pain. The zombified glob of what were once human beings, thrashed around the halted train car. Unable to move, unable to break free from the dark, my writing became more apparent as I stared into the facelessness of their crimson eyes. The eyes of a species that once looked up at the sky with wonder, spoke to the stars with humility, and danced atop towers of ice and rock with gratitude; was now a huddled mass of red pustule neophytes, clinging to the tracks of Nath'Zrath's demented railway, begging to find their way in a moment of desperate uncertainty.

OUR LADY OF HOLY DEATH

COLLEEN ANDERSON

Originally published in The Horror Writers Association Poetry Showcase Vol. IX

I am black blooming mushrooms and breath's foul decay. I am the night's cloak pulled tight, choking the light. I am crushed carapaces and the hiss of lightning striking true. I am blue-puce infection chewing through your meat. I am the soft wet thud of gun spray and ocean's ravenous reach. I care not whether you hide or face me. I am always here.

> locked doors and windows
> Autumn chills toward winter
> pathways lie open

Hold off the war, my Lady, keep death's perfume for midnight. Extinguish the bright kiss of vipers and wasps until summer's fruity cotillion. Let no bullet or knife choose to winter in me. Please drop your mantle over my affairs so they avoid detection's laser eye. Harbor my children in your arms so they may grow to see time crease their faces. I ask these gifts of you and will always be yours.

> cleaning out the house
> Spring promises strange new births
> vase of dried flowers

THE MEDIUM

Naching T. Kassa

Old woman clad in widow's weeds,
She glides across the floor,
Pale eyes shine sightless,
Warm blood flows,

She settles at the table,
Links cold hands with mine,
Candlewick flares white,
He screams in silence,

Silver hair neath gaslight glows,
She calls to tear the veil,
The spirit answers from beyond,
More than body broken and torn,

Why did they call her here?
This witch from ages past,
I thought she bore false witness,
Brick by brick I walled him in,

She convulses, my victim speaks,
My hand trapped in hers,
As she reveals my darkest secret,
The death which haunts me.

WHISPERS IN INK

ANGELA YURIKO SMITH

Always, the whispers fill my ears.
The inky spirits sneak in, invade my gray matter
and leave me trembling as pale as paper.
No rest until I scratch their voices into being.

The inky spirits sneak in, invade my gray matter
demanding ghosts of experience past.
No rest until I scratch their voices into being.
They insist on being heard and seen.

Demanding ghosts of experience past—
they guide my hand, the pen a planchette.
They insist on being heard and seen—
only fools refuse their muse.

They guide my hand, the pen a planchette
and leave me trembling as pale as paper.
Only fools refuse their muse.
Always, the whispers fill my ears.

THE END?

Not if you want to dive into more of Crystal Lake Publishing's Tales from the Darkest Depths!

Check out our amazing website and online store
or download our latest catalog here.
https://geni.us/CLPCatalog

Looking for award-winning Dark Fiction?
Download our latest catalog.

Includes our anthologies, novels, novellas, collections,
poetry, non-fiction, and specialty projects.

WHERE STORIES COME ALIVE!

We always have great new projects and content on the website to dive into, as well as a newsletter, behind the scenes options, social media platforms, our own dark fiction shared-world series and our very own webstore. Our webstore even has categories specifically for KU books, non-fiction, anthologies, and of course more novels and novellas.

More Poetry collections by Crystal Lake Publishing:

Readers . . .

Thank you for reading *Whispers from Beyond*. We hope you enjoyed this poetry collection.

If you have a moment, please review *Whispers from Beyond* at the store where you bought it.

Help other readers by telling them why you enjoyed this book. No need to write an in-depth discussion. Even a single sentence will be greatly appreciated. Reviews go a long way to helping a book sell, and is great for an author's career. It'll also help us to continue publishing quality books.

Thank you again for taking the time to journey with Crystal Lake Publishing.

Visit our Linktree page for a list of our social media platforms. https://linktr.ee/CrystalLakePublishing

Our Mission Statement:

Since its founding in August 2012, Crystal Lake Publishing has quickly become one of the world's leading publishers of Dark Fiction and Horror books. In 2023, Crystal Lake Publishing formed a part of Crystal Lake Entertainment, joining several other divisions, including Torrid Waters, Crystal Lake Comics, Crystal Lake Kids, and many more.

While we strive to present only the highest quality fiction and entertainment, we also endeavour to support authors along their writing journey. We offer our time and experience in non-fiction projects, as well as author mentoring and services, at competitive prices.

With several Bram Stoker Award wins and many other wins and nominations (including the HWA's Specialty Press Award), Crystal Lake Publishing puts integrity, honor, and respect at the forefront of our publishing operations.

We strive for each book and outreach program we spearhead to not only entertain and touch or comment on issues that affect our readers, but also to strengthen and support the Dark Fiction field and its authors.

Not only do we find and publish authors we believe are destined for greatness, but we strive to work with men and women who endeavour to be decent human beings who care more for others than themselves, while still being hard working, driven, and passionate artists and storytellers.

Crystal Lake Publishing is and will always be a beacon of what passion and dedication, combined with overwhelming teamwork and respect, can accomplish. We endeavour to know each and every one of our readers, while building personal relationships with our authors, reviewers, bloggers, podcasters, bookstores, and libraries.

We will be as trustworthy, forthright, and transparent as any business can be, while also keeping most of the headaches away from our authors, since it's our job to solve the problems so they can stay in a creative mind. Which of course also means paying our authors.

We do not just publish books, we present to you worlds within your world, doors within your mind, from talented authors who sacrifice so much for a moment of your time.

There are some amazing small presses out there, and through collaboration and open forums we will continue to support other presses in the goal of helping authors and showing the world what quality small presses are capable of accomplishing. No one wins when a small press goes down, so we will always be there to support hardworking, legitimate presses and their authors. We don't see Crystal Lake as the best press out there, but we will always strive to be the best, strive to be the most interactive and grateful, and even blessed press around. No matter what happens over time, we will also take our mission very seriously while appreciating where we are and enjoying the journey.

What do we offer our authors that they can't do for themselves through self-publishing?

We are big supporters of self-publishing (especially hybrid publishing), if done with care, patience, and planning. However, not every author has the time or inclination to do market research, advertise, and set up book launch strategies. Although a lot of authors are successful in doing it all, strong small presses will always be there for the authors who just want to do what they do best: write.

What we offer is experience, industry knowledge, contacts and trust built up over years. And due to our strong brand and trusting fanbase, every Crystal Lake Publishing book comes with weight of respect. In time our fans begin to trust our judgment and will try a new author purely based on our support of said author.

With each launch we strive to fine-tune our approach, learn from our mistakes, and increase our reach. We continue to assure our authors that we're here for them and that we'll carry the weight of the launch and dealing with third parties while they focus on their strengths—be it writing, interviews, blogs, signings, etc.

We also offer several mentoring packages to authors that

include knowledge and skills they can use in both traditional and self-publishing endeavours.

We look forward to launching many new careers.

This is what we believe in. What we stand for. This will be our legacy.

**Welcome to Crystal Lake Publishing—
Tales from the Darkest Depths.**